Buster

the Very Shy Dog

Finds a Kitten

by **Lisze Bechtold**

Green Light Readers

HOUGHTON MIFFLIN HARCOURT

Boston New York

For Marietta and Nancy, stalwart and intrepid —L.B.

Green Light Readers and its logo are trademarks of HMH Publishers LLC,
registered in the United States and other countries.

www.hmhco.com

The text of this book is set in Goudy.
The illustrations were drawn on a Cintiq computer tablet, then printed and painted with watercolors.

Library of Congress Cataloging-in-Publication Data
Bechtold, Lisze, author, illustrator.
Buster the very shy dog finds a kitten / by Lisze Bechtold.
p. cm.
Summary: Buster finds a homeless kitten and takes care of it, with help from Phoebe, the tabby, and the calico.
In a second story, Buster and Phoebe take the new kitten, Tilly, to Gregory's house to play.
ISBN 978-0-544-33605-6 paperback
ISBN 978-0-544-33604-9 paper over board
[1. Bashfulness—Fiction. 2. Dogs—Fiction. 3. Cats—Fiction. 4. Animals—Infancy—Fiction.] I. Title.
PZ7.B380765Bw 2015
[E]—dc23
2014006759

Manufactured in China
SCP 10 9 8 7 6 5 4 3 2 1

4500520606

CONTENTS

Buster the Very Shy Dog
Finds a Kitten

Buster and Phoebe were hiding.
They watched Roger's cats stroll by.
"Okay . . . now!" said Phoebe.
The two dogs jumped out.

The tabby cat ran.

Phoebe chased him.

"Ha! Ha! You can't catch me!" laughed the tabby cat.

The calico cat hissed.

Buster hid under the porch.
Then he heard a voice in the shadows.
Something scratched his nose.

"Yikes!" he cried.

He ran out from under the porch.

A tiny kitten followed him.

"Meeeee-ew," she said.

"What is wrong?" asked Buster.

"I'm hu-u-u-u-ngry," she said.

"Why don't you go home?" asked Buster.

"I don't have a home," said the kitten.

"You are too little to be all alone," said Buster.

He went into the house to look for food.
He found some food in the cat bowls.

Phoebe came over.
"What are you doing?" she asked.
"I'm feeding this baby cat," said Buster.

The cats came over.

"Hey! That's my bowl!" shouted the tabby cat.

"Ew! There is dog slobber in it," said the calico cat.

"Not my slobber," said Phoebe.

"Buster gave your food to that kitten."

"Go home! This is our yard," hissed the calico.

"Eat your own food," snapped the tabby cat.

The kitten trembled.

"Stop it!" barked Buster. "She doesn't have a home."
"Well, she is not moving in here," said Phoebe.
"Take her somewhere else," said the calico.
"And stay out of our food," warned the tabby cat.

"I will take care of you, Baby Cat," said Buster.
But he knew it would not be easy.

Nighttime was very cold.

The kitten shivered under the porch.

Buster lay down next to her.

He missed his cozy dog bed.

"I will sneak you into the house," Buster told her.

Buster hid the kitten in his dog bed.
But she did not stay there.
The kitten played with Phoebe's toys.
Phoebe frowned, then said, "She is kind of funny.
But don't let Roger see her."

The kitten napped in the calico's bed.
The calico frowned, then said, "She is kind of cute.
But don't let Roger see her."

The kitten gobbled up all of the tabby cat's food.
The tabby cat frowned, then said, "Wow! She eats a
lot. Don't let Roger see her."

Buster hid the kitten under a blanket.

"Buster, let's play," said Phoebe.

"Maybe later," said Buster. "I am watching Baby Cat."

"Come on, Buster — let's play now!" barked Phoebe.

She threw a ball.

The kitten chased after it . . .

. . . and bumped into Roger's shoes!

"Where did you come from?" said Roger.
The kitten squirmed in his hands.
"You look like one of the stray cats I saw yesterday,"
Roger said. The kitten mewed to Buster for help.

Buster barked, "Let Baby Cat live here.
I will take care of her!"
But Roger did not understand.

Buster stared at Roger.
Phoebe stared at Roger.
The cats stared at Roger.

At last, Roger understood.

"I guess we have a new cat in our family," he said.

"I'll name you Tilly."

"Hurray!" barked Buster.

"Now you'll get your own toys," said Phoebe.

"And your own bed," said the calico.

"And your own food dish," said the tabby cat.

"Wow!" said Tilly. "I will share them all."

And she did.

Tilly Meets Gregory

"Let's go play with Gregory," said Buster.

"Okay," said Phoebe. "Maybe he has a new bone."

Tilly followed them into Gregory's yard.

"Hey! No cats in my yard," barked Gregory.

"Tilly is just a baby cat," said Buster.

"Does she like to play chase-the-cat?" Gregory asked.

Buster shook his head no.

"Does she like to dig holes?" asked Gregory.

Tilly nodded her head yes.

"Good. Let's dig up a bone," said Gregory.

Phoebe licked her lips.

They began to dig.

Dirt flew everywhere.

"Here is the bone!" cried Phoebe.
They stopped digging.
"Where is Tilly?" asked Buster.
They looked around.

"I don't like digging," said a muffled voice.
Tilly shook the dirt from her fur.

"Let's play tug-the-rope," said Gregory.
Gregory and Phoebe pulled one end of the rope.
Buster and Tilly pulled the other end.

Gregory yanked the rope hard.

Buster and Tilly fell over.

"That was fun," said Buster.

"I don't like tug-the-rope, either," said Tilly.

"What do *you* want to do?" Buster asked.

"Let's watch birds," said Tilly.

They all watched birds.

"Ack, ack, ack, ack, ack," Tilly said softly to the birds.

"This is really boring," whispered Gregory.

"Let's talk to the birds like Tilly," said Buster.

"Ack, ack, ack, ack, ack," said Tilly.

"Arf, arf, arf, arf, arf!" said the dogs.

All the birds flew away.

"You were too loud," cried Tilly.

"Sorry," said Buster. "Let's catch bugs."

"I have an idea," said Gregory.

"Whoever finds the scariest bug gets the bone."

"Great idea!" said Phoebe.

She ran to the flower bed.

"Scariest bug?" said Buster.

How was he going to catch a scary bug?

Scary bugs were . . . *scary.*

Gregory knocked over the water bucket.
Bugs scurried everywhere.
Gregory and Tilly pounced on them.
Buster jumped back.

"Got one!" said Gregory.

"Got one!" said Tilly.

"I got one!" called Phoebe.

Buster decided to be brave.

He opened his mouth and closed his eyes.

He grabbed a bug.

It squeaked.

"Got one," he mumbled.

Phoebe came back with her bug.

"This is the hairiest bug ever," she said.

"I said *scariest*, not hairiest," said Gregory.

"Oh," said Phoebe.

Gregory showed his bug.

Buster backed away.

Tilly showed her bug.
Everyone jumped back.
"Wow, that is one scary bug!" said Gregory.

"Let's see your bug, Buster," said Tilly.

Buster opened his mouth.
A big blob of soggy fur fell out.
"That is scary," said Tilly.
"And very hairy," said Phoebe.

"But it is not a bug," said Gregory.
"It is the squeak toy I lost."

"Tilly wins the bone," said Gregory.
Tilly twirled.
Then Tilly tried to lift the bone.
It was way too big.

"Maybe I will just leave the bone here,"
said Tilly, "and visit it sometimes."
"Anytime," said Gregory.